KIDS AGAINST HUNGER

by Jon Mikkelsen

illustrated by Nathan Lueth

Librarian Reviewer

Marci Peschke

Librarian, Dallas Independent School District

MA Education Reading Specialist, Stephen F. Austin State University

Learning Resources Endorsement, Texas Women's University

Reading Consultant

Elizabeth Stedem

Educator/Consultant, Colorado Springs, CO

MA in Elementary Education, University of Denver, CO

STONE ARCH BOOKS

www.stonearchbooks.com

Keystone Books are published by Stone Arch Books
151 Good Counsel Drive, P.O. Box 669
Mankato, Minnesota 56002
www.stonearchbooks.com

Library of Congress Cataloging-in-Publication Data
Mikkelsen, Jon.
    Kids Against Hunger / by Jon Mikkelsen; illustrated by Nathan
Lueth.
        p. cm. — (Keystone Books. We Are Heroes)
        ISBN 978-1-4342-0790-6 (library binding)
        ISBN 978-1-4342-0886-6 (pbk.)
        [1. Voluntarism—Fiction.] I. Lueth, Nathan, ill. II. Title.
PZ7.M59268Ki 2009
[Fic]—dc22   2008008119

Summary: Greg skips soccer practice once a week. His teammates want
to find out why.

                    ,

Art Director: Heather Kindseth
Graphic Designer: Brann Garvey

*This book is dedicated to all of the men, women, and children who
have helped Kids Against Hunger™ fight against starvation.*

1 2 3 4 5 6 13 12 11 10 09 08

Printed in the United States of America

TABLE OF CONTENTS

Chapter 1

Chase loved one thing more than anything else in the whole world. Soccer.

He played it in the spring. He played it in the summer. He played it in the fall. And in the winter, when it was too cold to play outside, he went to an indoor soccer field that was near his house.

Soccer was Chase's favorite thing.

One sunny summer afternoon, Chase was on his way to practice. He saw his best friend, Ian.

"Hey, Ian!" Chase called.

"What's up, Chase?" said Ian.

"Are you excited to practice?" asked Chase.

"Yup," Ian replied. "I want to work on some passing drills."

Chase had started playing soccer when he was five years old. Now he was almost fourteen, and he was getting better all the time. But he wasn't as good as Ian.

"Drills are boring," said Chase. "But we're getting better. The extra practice must be paying off."

"I know," replied Ian. "But practicing all the time is killing me. My legs are still sore from Monday's practice."

"Race you to the field," Chase said. "Last one there is a rotten egg!" Then he took off as fast as he could.

"You're on!" shouted Ian. Then he sprinted after Chase.

Chapter 2

WHERE'S GREG?

When they got to the field, the other kids had already started their drills.

Coach Lopez blew his whistle when he saw Ian and Chase. "Let's get going!" Coach Lopez yelled. "Pair off and practice dribbling for ten yards. Then practice passing. Go!"

Then Deshawn Reynolds raised his hand. "Coach, I don't have a partner," Deshawn said.

"What?" the coach screamed. "That means someone didn't show up! Who isn't here? Who is your partner?"

Deshawn looked really scared. He whispered, "Greg Lewis."

The coach stopped looking mad. With a quieter voice, he said, "Oh. Well, that's fine. You can practice with me, Reynolds."

Coach Lopez picked up a ball. He and Deshawn headed across the field.

Chase and Ian started dribbling and passing.

"That's not fair," said Chase. "Greg always misses practice on Wednesday. Coach never says a word. If one of us did that, we'd get kicked off the team!"

"You got that right," replied Ian. "Or else Coach would make us run laps until we dropped. It's like Greg doesn't even care at all about the team."

"But he's still a good player," Chase said. "He was great in last week's game. I just don't understand why he can skip practice, but no one else ever can. It's not fair."

Ian shrugged his shoulders. He said, "Maybe Coach will say something to him."

"I doubt it," replied Chase. "He never does. Greg is Coach's favorite."

Ian nodded. "I know," he said. "There's something fishy about this."

Chapter 3

TEAMWORK

Chase showed up early to practice on Monday. Ian was already there, putting on his cleats. Then Greg walked up to the field.

"Well, well, well," Chase told Ian. "Look who made it. I'm going to say something to him."

Greg was stretching to warm up. Chase walked over to him. Greg said, "Hey, Chase. How's it going?"

"Hey, Greg," Chase said. "I was just wondering where you were during the practice on Wednesday."

Greg stared at the ground. "Uh," he stammered, "I had to, uh, do something."

"But we had practice," Chase said, narrowing his eyes. "I was here. Ian was here. Deshawn, your partner, was here. In fact, everyone else was here. But you weren't. Why didn't you show up, Greg? Don't you care about this team?"

Greg quickly stood up. He stared at Chase.

"Of course I care," Greg said. "And at least I scored a point at our last game. What did you do?"

Chase was starting to get really mad. He said, "You may have scored a point, but at least we believe in teamwork."

Greg took a step closer. "I believe in teamwork!" he said, louder.

"No you don't!" Chase yelled. "If you did, you would come to every practice! So what's your big excuse for missing practice?"

By this time, some of the other teammates noticed what was going on. They began to gather around.

Coach Lopez noticed the argument too. He ran over. Then he pulled the two angry guys away from each other. "All right, what's going on here?" the coach asked.

"Why?" asked Chase. "Why did you miss practice?"

Greg looked at Chase. Then he looked at Coach Lopez. Coach Lopez didn't say anything. Then Greg looked at the ground again. "It's none of your business," Greg said.

"Okay," said Coach Lopez. "Everyone get back on the field. Practice some goal kicks."

Everyone ran back onto the field except Chase and Ian.

"He's hiding something," said Chase.

"What could he be hiding?" Ian asked.

"I don't know," Chase said, "but I'm going to find out."

Chapter 4

FOLLOWING GREG

The next Wednesday, Chase told his coach that he wouldn't be at practice. He said that he and Ian had to stay after school and finish a project.

But there was no project. The boys went to Greg's house. They hid behind some bushes and waited.

"I never should have let you talk me into this," said Ian. "This is a bad idea."

Just then, the front door of Greg's house swung open.

Greg stepped outside. He looked up and down the street. Then he ran down the steps. He started jogging up the road. He was heading away from the practice field.

"See?" Chase whispered. "I told you. He's not going to soccer practice. Come on, let's follow him!"

Ian sighed, but he got up. They both jogged after Greg.

Chase and Ian followed him for what seemed like a mile.

Finally, they came to an old warehouse. Chase thought the building looked like it was haunted.

A sign above the front door was painted with the letters KAH. Greg took one final look around. Then he went inside.

"I suppose you're going to say we should follow him in there," said Ian.

"Yes," replied Chase. "I want to find out what could be so important that he would miss soccer practice."

"Fine," Ian said. "But you owe me."

They made sure no one could see
them. Then Chase and Ian opened the
creaky, rusted door. They walked inside
the mysterious building.

Inside the old warehouse, the halls were empty. Greg was nowhere to be seen.

"Look!" whispered Chase. "Down that way!" He pointed down the hall. There was light shining through a set of double doors.

"He's got to be in there," said Chase. He headed down the hall.

"Wait up!" Ian whispered loudly.

Chase and Ian crept down the hall toward the doors. The glass in the doors was dirty. When they pressed their faces to the glass, they could see inside the room.

Greg was inside the room. There were other kids there too. They were each wearing gray things over their clothes.

"What are those things they're wearing?" Ian whispered.

"I don't know," Chase replied. "They look like aprons."

"And they're wearing gloves. Wait a second. Is he wearing a hairnet?" Ian asked.

"Yeah, it looks like it," Chase said.

Greg stood behind a table.

There was a big sack on the table.
He scooped some yellow powder from
the sack. He put the powder into a
plastic bag. Then he passed the bag to
the girl standing next to him.

"What are they doing?" asked Ian. "What is that yellow powder?"

Chase said, "I don't know. Maybe this is some kind of lab, and they're mixing dangerous chemicals together."

Ian replied, "Dangerous chemicals? What would they be doing with dangerous chemicals?"

"I don't know," Chase said. "Something dangerous?"

Just then, they heard a voice behind them. "Hey! What are you kids doing?"

ALL THE HELP WE CAN GET

A tall man wearing a white coat walked over to Chase and Ian.

"Uh, we aren't doing anything," Chase said. "We were just leaving."

"Leaving?" said the tall man. "No, you can't leave! We need all the help we can get." He opened the doors and pushed the boys into the room. Everyone in the room stopped and looked at them.

Greg looked surprised. "Chase? Ian? What are you two doing here?" he asked.

"Uh, nothing," Chase lied. "We were just looking for the bathroom. Ian had to go."

"Hey! I did not! It was all Chase's idea!" Ian said.

"You two followed me here, didn't you?" said Greg. "You were spying on me!"

Chase shook his head and said, "No, we weren't! We just wanted to know why you kept missing practice."

Greg shook his head. "I told you that was none of your business," he said angrily. "But if you have to know, I'm volunteering."

"What do you mean?" asked Ian.

"I come here on Wednesdays to help Kids Against Hunger," Greg said.

"What's Kids Against Hunger?" Chase asked, confused.

"It's a group that helps feed hungry people all over the world," Greg explained.

28

The tall man nodded. He said, "I'm Tom, the local director of the group. We have kids help us out. They put this rice casserole powder into bags. Then we send the packages all over the world."

Chase looked at the sack on the table next to Greg. "That's what that yellow stuff is? Rice casserole powder?" Chase asked.

"Yeah," said Greg. "What did you think it was?" He laughed, and added, "Something dangerous?"

"I still don't get it," Chase said. "I mean, I get that you're volunteering here. But that means you miss half of our soccer practices. Why don't you just quit one or the other?"

"I made a deal with Coach Lopez," Greg explained quietly. "I told him what I was doing here. I also agreed to come to an extra practice every Saturday with him one on one. That way, I won't get rusty. I won't let the team down."

Chase felt relieved, but he was still confused. "But why did you keep it a secret?" he asked. "Why didn't you just tell us?"

Greg looked down at the ground. He said quietly, "When I was little, my family didn't have a lot of money. Sometimes we were hungry. It's not something I like to talk about. Things are better for us now, but I still wanted to help kids who are hungry, like I used to be."

Chase walked over to Greg and stuck out his hand. "I'm sorry," he said. "You weren't letting the team down. I'm sorry I didn't believe in you."

Greg smiled. He shook Chase's hand. "Well, I wish you would have believed me, but thanks for saying you're sorry," Greg said.

"I have a great idea," Ian said. "Why don't we ask Coach Lopez to change our practice day to Thursday? Then on Wednesdays, the whole team can come here to help out."

Tom smiled and said, "I love that idea. In fact, if you're not busy now, you can start today!"

"Really?" asked Chase. "What can we do?"

"There's lots you can do," Tom told him. "Wait here, and I'll grab some aprons, gloves, and hairnets for you."

Ian frowned. "We have to wear hairnets?" he asked.

Greg smiled. "Yep," he said. "We always say we look like lunch ladies. But it's worth it!"

ABOUT THE AUTHOR

Jon Mikkelsen has written dozens of plays for kids, which have involved aliens, superheroes, and more aliens. He acts on stage and loves performing in front of an audience. Jon also loves sushi, cheeseburgers, and pizza. He loves to travel, and has visited Moscow, Berlin, London, and Amsterdam. He lives in Minneapolis and has a cat named Coco, who does not pay rent.

ABOUT THE ILLUSTRATOR

Nathan Lueth has been a freelance illustrator since 2004. He graduated from the Minneapolis College of Art and Design in 2004, and has done work for companies like Target, General Mills, and Wreked Records. Nathan was a 2008 finalist in Tokyopop's Rising Stars of Manga contest. He lives in Minneapolis, Minnesota.

GLOSSARY

argument (AR-gyoo-muhnt)—a disagreement

chemicals (KEM-uh-kuhlz)—substances used in chemistry

cleats (KLEETS)—special shoes worn to play soccer

dangerous (DAYN-jur-uhss)—likely to cause harm

drills (DRILLZ)—doing something over and over to learn how to do it better

excuse (ek-SKYOOSS)—a reason you give to explain why you have done something wrong

hairnet (HAIR-net)—a net worn over the hair to make sure that no hair falls into food

mysterious (miss-TEER-ee-uhss)—hard to explain

practice (PRAK-tiss)—getting together as a team to work on skills

volunteer (vol-uhn-TEER)—do something without pay

warehouse (WAIR-hous)—a large building used for storing goods

DISCUSSION QUESTIONS

1. Why were Ian and Chase mad that Greg was missing practice?

2. Greg missed practice to volunteer, even though he loved soccer. Would you skip doing your favorite thing to help others? Why or why not?

3. Did Ian and Chase do the right thing when they followed Greg to the warehouse? What would you have done?

WRITING PROMPTS

1. Have you ever volunteered? What did you do? If you haven't, what is something you would like to do as a volunteer?

2. Sometimes it's interesting to think about a story from another person's point of view. Try writing chapter 5 from Greg's point of view. What does he see and hear? What does he think about? How does he feel?

3. At the end of this book, the boys plan to ask their coach to let the whole team volunteer. Write a chapter that tells what happens when the team volunteers for Kids Against Hunger.

MORE ABOUT KIDS AGAINST HUNGER™

Kids Against Hunger™ is a nonprofit organization whose mission is to help end starvation. Twelve children die every minute of starvation or diseases related to not having the right nutrition, and Kids Against Hunger™ works to try to end that problem.

Kids Against Hunger™ was founded in 1999 by a man named Richard Proudfit. In 1974, Richard traveled on a medical mission to Honduras, where he saw the effects of Hurricane Fifi. Many children were dying of starvation. Richard decided that he needed to try to help.

Richard knew that he needed to find a way to get healthy, nutritious food to children who needed it. He talked to executives at Cargill, Pillsbury, General Mills, and Archer Daniels Midland to help him create the right food. They created the Rice-Soy Casserole. It includes vegetables, protein, carbohydrates, and vitamins, all of which are needed for healthy, growing kids' bodies.

The next step was getting the food to the kids who need it.

To save on the costs of producing and packaging the food, so that more money can go directly to making food for the kids who need it, Kids Against Hunger™ relies on volunteers. Kids and adults of all ages work in fourteen states and Canada to package the food. Then it is shipped around the world.

The food packaged by Kids Against Hunger™ is shipped to more than 40 countries worldwide through a network of governments, churches, and other nonprofit organizations. Recently, more than one million meals were sent to the area devastated by Hurricane Katrina.

It costs Kids Against Hunger™ about 23 cents to make each meal. That money is donated by people all over the world to help feed children who are starving.

To learn more about Kids Against Hunger™, go to www.feedingchildren.org.

INTERNET SITES

Do you want to know more about subjects related to this book? Or are you interested in learning about other topics? Then check out FactHound, a fun, easy way to find Internet sites.

Our investigative staff has already sniffed out great sites for you!

Here's how to use FactHound:

1. Visit *www.facthound.com*

2. Select your grade level.

3. To learn more about subjects related to this book, type in the book's ISBN number: **9781434207906**.

4. Click the **Fetch It** button.

FactHound will fetch the best Internet sites for you!